The Seventh Well